'We've got to do something!' James shouted as he reached his friend. 'The ghosts are behind this!'

'Muh!' groaned Lenny.

'Muh?' repeated James. 'What's "Muh"?'

'Don't feel well,' said Lenny, weakly. 'Too many pies.'

'Never mind that!' snapped James. 'We've got to do something!' He grabbed Lenny's wrist and tried to pull him to his feet but his friend just slid down and pressed his face against the cold, wet concrete of the playground.

'Lenny! I saw some ghosts go into the ghost train. We have to keep them trapped in there!' James's eyes widened as an idea hit him. 'Trap the ghosts . . . That's it!' He sprinted back towards the sports field and the science invention contest.

There's only one person who can help me now, he thought. *And he's dressed as a jester!*

**St Sebastian's School in Grimesford
is the pits. No, really — it is.**

Every year, the high school sinks a bit further into
the boggy plague pit beneath it and, every year, the
ghosts of the plague victims buried underneath it
become a bit more cranky.

Egged on by their spooky ringleader, Edith Codd,
they decide to get their own back — and they're
willing to play dirty. *Really* dirty.

They kick up a stink by causing as much mischief
as in inhumanly possible so as to get St Sebastian's
closed down once and for all.

But what they haven't reckoned on is year-seven
new boy, James Simpson and his friends Alexander
and Lenny.

The question is, are the gang up to the challenge
of laying St Sebastian's paranormal problem to rest,
or will their school remain forever frightful?

There's only one way to find out . . .

www.too-ghoul.com

A Fête Worse Than Death

B. STRANGE

EGMONT

Special thanks to:

Tommy Donbavand, St John's Walworth Church of England Primary School and Belmont Primary School

EGMONT

We bring stories to life

Published in Great Britain 2008
by Egmont UK Limited
239 Kensington High Street, London W8 6SA

Text & illustrations © 2008 Egmont UK Ltd
Text by Tommy Donbavand
Illustrations by Pulsar Studios

ISBN 978 1 4052 3927 1

1 3 5 7 9 10 8 6 4 2

A CIP catalogue record for this title is available
from the British Library

Typeset by Avon DataSet Ltd, Bidford on Avon, Warwickshire
Printed and bound in Great Britain by the CPI Group

School versus...

Leader of the pack and general, all-round good guy

James Simpson

Brain the size of a planet - and database of bad jokes to match

Alexander Tick

Food rules his head, but animals rule his heart. Ahhh...

Lenny Maxwell

...Ghoul!

This haggy old ghost doesn't think children should be seen OR heard!

Edith Codd

Spooky school saviour or disobedient little meddler? - you decide

William Scroggins

The only ghost ever to have a working digestive system

Ambrose Harbottle

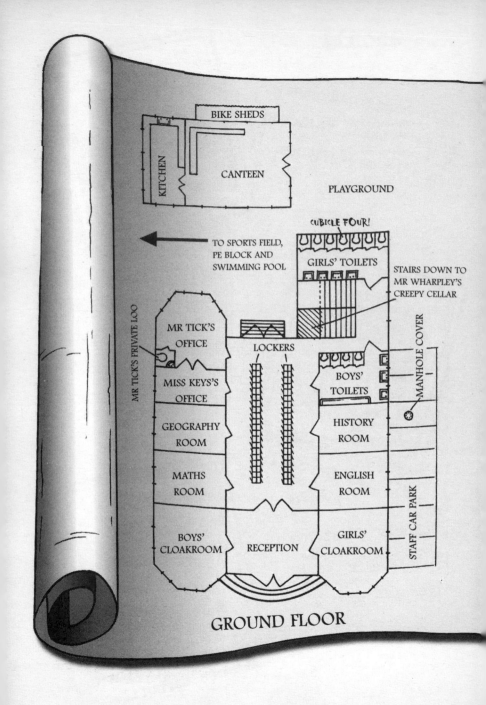

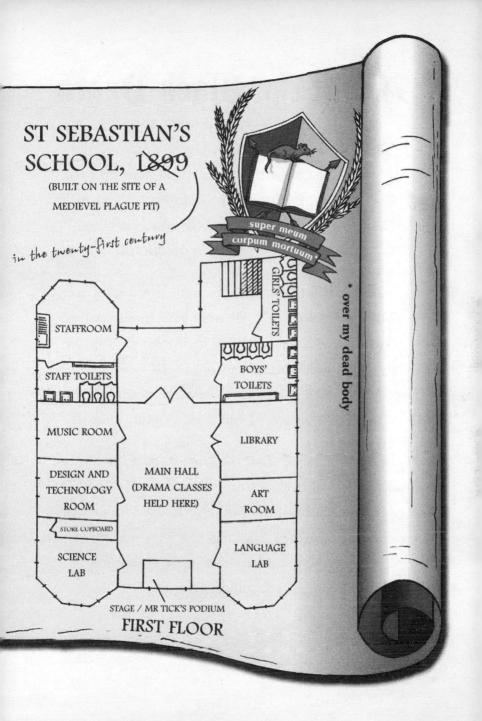

About the Black Death

The Black Death was a terrible plague that
is believed to have been spread by fleas on rats.
It swept through Europe in the fourteenth century,
arriving in England in 1348, where it killed
over one third of the population.

One of the Black Death's main symptoms was
**foul-smelling boils all over the body called
'buboes'.** The plague was so infectious that its
victims and their families were locked in their houses
until they died. Many villages were abandoned as
the disease wiped out their populations.

So many people died that graveyards overflowed
and bodies lay in the street, so special **'plague pits'**
were dug to bury the bodies. Almost every town
and village in England has a plague pit
somewhere underneath it, so watch out
when you're digging in the garden . . .

Dear Reader

As you may have already guessed, B. Strange is not a real name.

The author of this series is an ex-teacher who is currently employed by a little-known body called the Organisation For Spook Termination (Excluding Demons), or O.F.S.T.(E.D.). 'B. Strange' is the pen name chosen to protect his identity.

Together, we felt it was our duty to publish these books, in an attempt to save innocent lives. The stories are based on the author's experiences as an O.F.S.T.(E.D.) inspector in various schools over the past two decades.

Please read them carefully - you may regret it if you don't . . .

Yours sincerely
The Publisher.

PS - Should you wish to file a report on any suspicious supernatural occurrences at your school, visit www.too-ghoul.com and fill out the relevant form. We'll pass it on to O.F.S.T.(E.D.) for you.

PPS - All characters' names have been changed to protect the identity of the individuals. Any similarity to actual persons, living or undead, is purely coincidental.

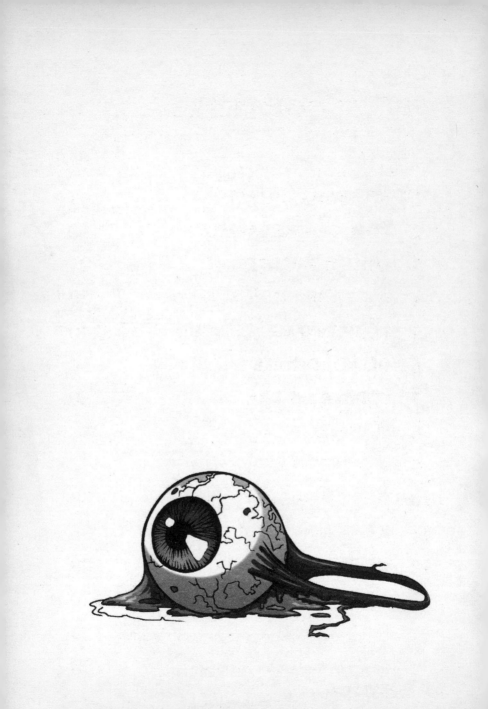

CONTENTS

1   NEW BAILS, PLEASE   1

2   ROLL OUT THE BARREL   10

3   LOVE AT FIRST FRIGHT   21

4   IT'S ALL IN THE PLANNING   30

5   FROM FUNFAIR TO UNFAIR   40

6   DO NOT DISTURB   50

7   TODAY'S THE DAY   60

8   SQUEEEEEZE   69

9   AND THEY'RE OFF!   78

10   DON'T PANIC!   88

11   JESTER MINUTE   98

12   WE'RE CAUGHT IN A TRAP   109

13   MONEY, MONEY, MONEY   120

EXTRA! FACT FILE, JOKES AND YUCKY STUFF   129

WHICH WITCH? SNEAK PREVIEW   136

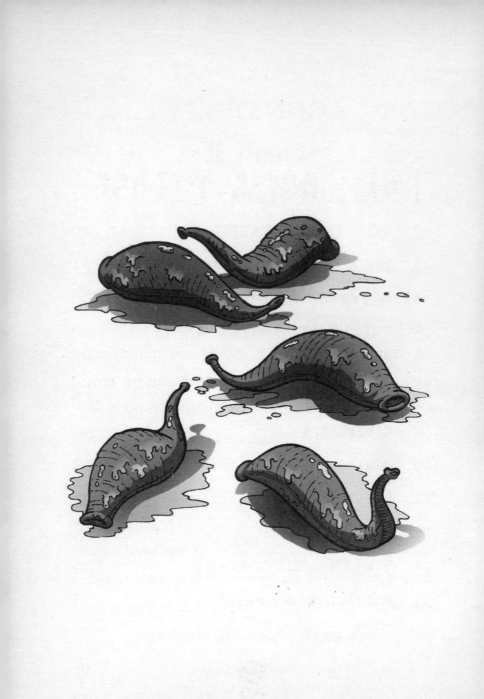

CHAPTER 1
NEW BALLS, PLEASE

'Lenny, Lenny! To me!'

Lenny Maxwell leapt into the air and punched the volleyball across the court towards his friend and teammate James Simpson. With only one point between the teams, this would be the shot that finally drew year-seven's Thunderbolts level with their year-eight rival team, The Stingrays.

James flicked his floppy brown fringe out of his eyes and launched himself off the ground in a jump timed perfectly to achieve the maximum height as the ball sailed towards him. Just a

metre away, over the net, Jason Yates also
jumped, arms raised to try and block James's
return shot.

The two athletes' eyes met. Both were
determined to win this rally and claim victory
for their team. And both knew whatever
happened next would change the outcome of the

match, and the St Sebastian's boys' volleyball league.

Alexander Tick dashed into position beside James, fists clenched to return any smash that Jason might be about to make. He gritted his teeth and watched as, almost in slow motion, the volleyball spun through the air and hung, for the briefest of moments, directly over James's head.

Jason could only stare as James's right hand whipped up from his side and lashed out for the ball. Skin made contact with leather as the Thunderbolts' top scorer smashed his palm into the ball . . . and the ball exploded, wrapping James's whole fist with what was left of the warm, sweat-soaked piece of sports equipment.

'Eurgh! Get it off!' wailed James, crashing back to the floor and shaking his hand to try and free it.

Lenny ran over and peeled the dead ball from his friend's fingers.

'Looks like the sticking plaster covering the puncture came unstuck,' said Alexander, trotting across the sports hall to the equipment cupboard to find the first-aid kit. 'I'll get another one.'

Carefully opening the battered old tin so as not to disturb its flaking paint, he rooted through its contents.

'There aren't any left!' he called over, to the disappointment of the volleyball players. 'Just an old, brown bandage and a bottle of painkillers filled with gummy bears.'

'Gummy bears?' questioned Lenny. 'What use are they if you've got an injury?'

'Actually, the effects of placebo medicines are well documented,' replied Alexander, as he rejoined his teammates. 'The psychosomatic results they achieve can often be compared favourably to those of genuine pharmaceutical products.'

Lenny blinked. 'Why don't you ever talk properly?' he asked.

James smiled. 'What Stick means is that if you just think you're taking a painkiller, it sometimes has the same effect as actually taking one.'

Lenny rubbed at his forehead. 'In that case, hand me the gummy bears; I'm getting a headache just listening to him.'

The peep of a whistle interrupted James's laugh as Ms Legg, the PE teacher, strode across the sports hall towards the two teams. 'Why have you boys stopped playing?' she demanded.

Alexander held up the remains of the volleyball. 'Problem with the equipment, miss,' he said. 'Have we got another one?'

Ms Legg shook her head. 'The only things left in the equipment cupboard are an oval hula hoop and a couple of bamboo garden canes we've been using for javelins.'

'And don't forget the vaulting horse that's so past its prime it's been put out to grass!' quipped Alexander, glancing from blank face to blank

5

face as he searched for someone who'd share
what he thought passed for a joke.

Ms Legg sighed. 'I swear, if you weren't the
headmaster's son we'd have buried you in the
long-jump pit months ago,' she mumbled under
her breath. 'Right!' she continued, pausing to let
loose another sharp blast on her whistle to get
everyone's attention. 'Consider this game
cancelled; you can fill the remaining lesson time
by doing laps of the sports hall.'

Ignoring the groans of 'Oh, miss!', Ms Legg
marched purposefully out of the sports hall. The
neglect of the PE department had gone on for
long enough.

When the telephone rang, Miss Keys, the school
secretary, jumped and pricked her finger for the
fifteenth time that morning.

She sighed and put down her needle and thread. Some of these lab coats were simply beyond repair; why couldn't Mr Tick just accept the fact? As much as she admired him, sometimes the headmaster could be a real penny-pincher.

After the phone conversation, Miss Keys buzzed through to the headmaster on the intercom – although intercom was a rather flattering description for the recently replaced system. What sat on Miss Keys's desk was one half of a second-hand baby monitor with the words 'Daddy's Little Princess' scribbled out with marker pen.

'Yes, Miss Keys?' droned the headmaster's voice through the tiny speaker, making the pink bunny on the front of the monitor light up. 'I'm at an important stage in my solitaire game right now. Can this wait?'

'I'm afraid not, Mr Tick,' replied the secretary.

'Ms Legg has telephoned to ask for some new sports equipment.'

'What?!' roared the pink bunny. 'Does she think I'm made of money?'

'That's not all, sir,' continued Miss Keys. 'I've also had calls this morning from Mr Drew saying the piano's got so many keys missing that the school orchestra can't follow the tune he's playing; Mr Parker wanting new batteries for the maths department's only calculator; and Mr Hall demanding to know why the new history textbooks you bought suddenly stop after the Battle of Hastings.'

Mr Tick appeared in the doorway that linked his office to the secretary's.

'This is ridiculous!' he snapped. 'Whatever happened to the days when all you needed to be a teacher was a piece of chalk and a can-do attitude?'

'They ended when these lab coats were in

fashion, sir,' smiled Miss Keys, as she stitched what had been part of a tablecloth on to one of the long, pointy collars.

It was obvious from Mr Tick's expression that he failed to see the joke.

'If we need extra money, why don't we hold some sort of school fête?' suggested Miss Keys. 'We could sell home-made plum jam and have a three-legged race!'

Mr Tick nodded slowly. 'The idea has merit,' he agreed, 'despite your talk of tasteless jam and stupid races. But it all just seems a lot of hard work which, frankly, I'm too important to be bothered with!'

Then a sly smile lit up the headmaster's face. 'However, the pupils aren't important at all. They shall organise the fête!'

CHAPTER 2
ROLL OUT THE BARREL

'What,' demanded Mr Tick with barely disguised disgust as the stage curtain was pulled back with a flourish, 'is that?'

'It's the tombola you asked me to make, sir!' insisted Mr Wharpley, pulling a dirty cloth from the pocket of his equally dirty caretaker's overalls and polishing the monstrosity that sat on the main hall stage.

'No . . .' said Mr Tick, slowly. 'It's an old oil barrel that you've covered in vomit-green paint and mounted on a rickety wooden frame.'

'Don't forget the nuts and bolts!' said Mr
Wharpley, proudly pointing out the handful of
odd-sized bits of metal painstakingly glued to
the barrel at random intervals.

'And they are for . . .?'

Mr Wharpley pressed a hand to the surface of
the barrel and spun it. 'They make it sparkle in
the light!' he announced.

Mr Tick's dark expression blackened even further. 'If that's all we've got, the children will just have to place their ideas for the fête in there.' He turned and strode away, adding: 'If you've put a slot in the drum, of course.'

Mr Wharpley's smile froze on his face. Stopping the barrel with one hand, he pulled a hacksaw from his toolbox with the other.

'I hate you, Tick . . .' he mumbled under his breath as he began to cut into the metal.

'And the first suggestion is . . .' announced Mr Tick, as he carefully slid his fingers past the razor-sharp metal edges of the slot cut into the tombola drum. 'A pelt-the-teachers-with-wet-sponges stall!'

A cheer went up around the hall as the headmaster scanned the rows of pupils for the note's author. 'Thank you, James Simpson,' he said as everyone in year seven tried to pat James on the back at the same time.

'Next . . .' Mr Tick gingerly pushed his arm back into the drum to pull out another sheet of paper, 'a competition for the most scientific invention!'

The cheers quickly faded to a chorus of hisses and comments such as, 'I know who that was!' and 'Stupid Stick!'

'I don't get it!' moaned Alexander to James. 'You suggest throwing damp bathroom products at the staff and you're treated like a hero. Yet when I attempt to further the cause of scientific achievement, I'm booed like a pantomime baddie!'

'I think,' grinned James, 'that you may have underestimated the gladiatorial nature of your fellow pupils.'

'What?' asked Lenny, glancing round to check he wasn't being watched by any teachers as he popped a handful of sweets into his mouth.

'We're a violent bunch!' explained James.

'Speaking of violent,' said Alexander, 'Carver's paying an awful lot of interest in all this. You don't think he's put a suggestion in, do you?'

James and Lenny followed Alexander's gaze to where Gordon 'The Gorilla' Carver was sitting. The school bully was watching carefully as Mr Tick's hand plunged back into the lime-green barrel.

'I'm not sure The Gorilla's the school-fête type,' said James.

Lenny snorted back a laugh. 'Yeah,' he said; 'what's he going to suggest? A smack-everyone-round-the-back-of-the-head stall?'

As the pupils sitting near Lenny giggled at the idea, Mr Tick opened the next piece of paper. 'I'm delighted to see that Gordon Carver has decided to become involved,' the headmaster announced. Lenny's eyes widened. 'It's quite difficult to read his handwriting,' continued Mr Tick, 'but I think this says "punch everyone".'

Alexander, James and Lenny exchanged worried glances as Gordon turned to grin wickedly at the trio.

'A superb proposal!' announced Mr Tick.

'What?!' demanded Alexander out loud. 'How can you say that, Dad?'

Mr Tick fixed his son with a glare. 'Alexander,' he thundered, 'may I remind you that, between the hours of nine in the morning and three-twenty in the afternoon, I am *not* your father, but your *headmaster!*'

Alexander blushed as laughter rippled through the hall.

'Furthermore,' continued Mr Tick, 'Gordon has entered into the true spirit of the school fête. I think a delicious glass of fruit punch is just what everyone will need if the weather turns out to be as pleasant as we hope.' The headmaster's face cracked into an awkward smile. Appearing friendly to pupils was not something that came naturally to him.

'Old family recipe is it, Gordon?' he asked. 'I do hope there's cranberry juice in it. Nothing like a refreshing glass of cranberry punch!'

'No!' blurted out the bully, his face reddening with rage. 'I meant —'

But it was too late, Mr Tick had already pulled another slip of paper out of the barrel and was unfolding it.

Gordon spun and glared back across the rows of seated pupils to where James, Alexander and Lenny were toasting him with imaginary glasses.

At the back of the main hall, unnoticed by any of the pupils or staff, a thin stream of ectoplasm forced itself out through the broken thermostat of an ancient radiator.

Glancing round to check that no one was watching, the ectoplasm began to change shape and, within a few seconds, there was an extra boy sitting in assembly.

William Scroggins smiled to himself. He loved taking part in school activities and there was no reason that a little problem like having been dead for over six hundred years should stop him from doing so.

Having died from the bubonic plague at the age of eleven, and worked on his parents' land before that, William had never been given the chance to go to school. Now he was making up for lost time, and having the time of his death doing it.

He crossed his fingers tightly as Mr Tick continued to read suggestions for the school fête as they were pulled from the tombola drum:

Stacey Carmichael requested a beauty pageant, while her best friend and Lenny's sister, Leandra, wanted a splat-the-rat stall.

More ideas came: a cake sale, a ghost ride and face-painting. With each piece of paper Mr Tick pulled from the barrel, William squeezed his fingers together tighter. He knew it had been a big risk to put a suggestion in the barrel himself, and he'd had to do it late at night after the school was closed so that he wouldn't be seen. But he loved fairs and festivals so much that he just had to get involved.

'This looks like the last suggestion,' said Mr Tick as he pulled a ragged scrap of paper past the sharp, metal jaws of the barrel. Gripping the note with his fingertips, he sniffed at the paper and pulled a face. 'And may I remind all pupils that the use of fresh stationery is always preferable.'

William held his breath or, at least, he would have done if he hadn't stopped breathing six

centuries ago. This was it – his idea for the
school fête! Unable to write, he'd had to draw it
with a broken pencil on the back of an essay
about the Amazon rainforest that had been
flushed down the year-nine toilets three weeks
ago. But Mr Tick was about to consider his
suggestion.

'This looks like a scribbled drawing of a clown,' sneered Mr Tick, 'but it might as well go in. The school fête will have a court jester.'

At the back of the hall, William Scroggins decided that this was the best day of his death, *ever*.

CHAPTER 3
LOVE AT FIRST FRIGHT

Ambrose Harbottle leant back against the old, upturned barrel and pulled a wriggling leech out of his waistcoat pocket. He held it up to the gloomy light that seeped into the vast, underground amphitheatre dug out beneath the school and watched the creature squirm.

Life had been good to Ambrose, even if death hadn't been quite so kind. Before the plague had ended it, Ambrose had enjoyed a successful career as a leech merchant. Medical practice had advanced to such a stage that leeches were in high demand; used by doctors to cure everything from the common cold to stepping on a rusty nail.

Ambrose had been left a ramshackle old house by his uncle which, while in a dreadful state of disrepair, did have one big plus point for him: it was damp. The damp attracted the leeches and they started to breed. Soon, Ambrose was surrounded by the slimy creatures. They clung to his curtains, swarmed over his chairs and, each night, his bed was a seething mass of brown stickiness.

To anyone else, this would have been a disgusting way to live. But Ambrose knew that leeches were, to the right person, worth as much as gold. He was soon supplying surgeries far and wide, and even looking into the possibility of exporting his leeches abroad.

Nothing, however, had prepared Ambrose for the day he first tasted a leech. He was just packing a box of extra-large specimens, ready to be shipped to a hospital in North Grimesford, when he yawned, long and hard. Whether the leech in question had a suicide wish or just saw the man's mouth as an extra-damp cave to nap in, Ambrose would never be certain. What he did know was that, as the yawn progressed, one of the leeches slithered up his arm, across his shoulder and over his bottom lip.

Ambrose had panicked at first, choking as he tried to spit the leech out. But then, as it slithered down his throat and into his stomach, he realised that the taste of the creature was not entirely unpleasant. And it had left behind a slimy residue that added to the tangy aftertaste.

Cautiously, Ambrose reached into the box and picked up another leech. Should he try again? Would he be able to watch as he lowered the creature into his open mouth? And, more importantly, was he going to vomit all down his best tabard?

Screwing his eyes closed, Ambrose popped the leech into his mouth and sucked it down his throat. A smile crept across his face. This leech was even tastier than the first. Within minutes, Ambrose was digging his hands into the rapidly emptying box and shovelling fistfuls of leeches into his mouth. Plus, he found that, if he chewed, the leeches burst and released a soft, gooey centre. Ambrose had discovered his passion.

Now, six hundred years later and sitting in a puddle of what he hoped was mud beneath St Sebastian's School, the ghost of Ambrose Harbottle prepared to indulge his passion yet again. This tiny leech was no match for those he had bred during his lifetime, but it was still juicy, plump and sure to be filled with chewy goodness. He lowered the creature on to his waiting tongue.

A fist slammed down on to the barrel he was leaning against, and his arm was jolted, causing

Ambrose to throw the leech across the
amphitheatre, where it disappeared under a rock.

'I'll *kill* him!' screeched the owner of the fist.

Ambrose didn't need to look to see who it was
who had ruined his lunch, but that wasn't the
real reason he didn't turn around. Edith Codd,
the leader of the plague-pit ghosts, was as ugly

as she was angry. Although the contents of his stomach were now made of ectoplasm, he had no desire to bring them up and spoil a perfectly good tabard.

'William Scroggins has been back up to the school again!' roared Edith, kicking the barrel and finally shattering Ambrose's hope of a peaceful morning. 'I'll kill the little toad!'

Ambrose sighed. 'You can't kill William, Edith, he's been dead for as long as we have.'

The amphitheatre was flooded with silence. Ambrose stiffened. If things were bad when Edith shouted, they were a lot worse when she stopped. Cautiously, he peered around the edge of the barrel . . .

A foot clad in a filthy shoe made contact with Ambrose's chin and he performed an impressive backwards roll down the steps that led up to the barrel. 'Don't you dare be cheeky with me, Ambrose Harbottle!' yelled Edith. 'No ghost is

allowed to visit the school without my
permission!'

Edith brought her fist down on the barrel
again to make her point but, this time, her hand
went straight through the rotting, damp wood.
The hag watched in horror as the metal ring
surrounding the barrel pinged off and, one by
one, the planks at the sides collapsed inwards.
Edith's barrel was wrecked.

Several minutes later, Edith Codd was squeezing
her way up the pipe she'd spotted a happy,
singing William emerge from earlier that day.
Sliding through the dank, rust-coloured water
did little to improve her mood.

That barrel had been her ranting post for
almost five hundred years, ever since she had first
ordered the plague-pit ghosts to dig out the

amphitheatre beneath the school. From that barrel she had issued plans, promised victories and battled to inspire the pack of lazy spirits she was condemned to spend her death with. Now it was gone. Someone had to pay.

'Whatever has made you so happy, William Scroggins, I shall find and destroy it!' she cackled as she squeezed out of the broken valve that the younger ghost had slipped back through at the end of assembly.

Forcing herself into her scrawny human form, Edith shook drops of dirty water from her frizzy, matted, ginger hair and gazed around the main hall for anything that might have given an eleven-year-old ghost a brief moment of joy.

Then she saw it. Sitting on the small, raised stage was a metal barrel, painted in the most beautiful green that Edith had ever seen. It was studded with nuts and bolts that shone like diamonds, and the ragged slot in its side seemed to be smiling at her, begging her to come closer.

For the first time since she had died, Edith's eyes sparkled. 'That's the most beautiful barrel I've ever seen in my death,' she whispered.

CHAPTER 4
IT'S ALL IN THE PLANNING

Mr Wharpley dropped to the floor and shuffled forwards on his belly like a sniper. If Mr Thomas, the drama teacher, saw him his plan would be ruined. Slithering under a row of desks, the caretaker cursed silently as the spanner hanging from his tool belt clinked against the metal leg of a chair.

Mr Thomas's head snapped up and he scanned the room, empty of pupils since the lunchtime bell had rung. It was bad enough that he had to teach drama in a normal classroom on the mornings that Mr Tick held assembly, but now they were making him cram all his school play costumes and scenery in there with him.

Stacked all around were huge wooden boards decorated with painted castle corridors, plastic bats and black capes Miss Keys had made from a set of old curtains. Proud as he was of the script he had written for this year's production – *I Was a Vampire eBayer* – he had to admit that the props were starting to freak him out a bit. Take that giant rubber spider sitting on the desk in front of him, for example. Creepy-looking thing, that.

Mr Wharpley stayed still until he was certain that Mr Thomas had gone back to marking his essays, then he began to edge himself forwards once more. He'd presumed his involvement with the school fête had ended once he'd built the tombola drum, but he hadn't counted on the headmaster being quite such a skinflint.

'There's no point spending good money on hiring a ghost train for the pupils to ride on when you can knock one up for us!' Mr Tick had said at the last staff meeting. How was he supposed to do that? 'Knock up' a ghost train? There were tracks, carriages, lights and more to consider. Stupid, stupid Tick!

Of course, there'd been no money available for this massive project, so Mr Wharpley had no choice but to steal items from around the school – and that giant rubber spider was just what he needed!

Not moving his gaze from Mr Thomas, the caretaker slid himself under the first row of desks and felt about for the spider with his hand. Was that a leg? It certainly felt rubbery and hairy, but that could just as easily mean he had hold of one of the canteen hotdogs that a pupil had taken to class to munch on. Yes, there were other legs next to it. He had hold of the spider and, best of all, it was obscuring his hand from the drama teacher's view. Very slowly, Mr Wharpley began to pull it towards the edge of the desk.

Out of the corner of his eye, Mr Thomas saw the giant spider begin to move. His red pen paused over an essay. Yes – the spider was definitely moving!

As Mr Wharpley pulled the rubber spider to the floor, Mr Thomas pushed aside his pile of exercise books and leapt on to his desk, screaming like a vampire with toothache.

Mr Wharpley smiled to himself. A new prop for the ghost train, and a terrified teacher into the bargain. This was turning out to be a good day after all!

'Who voted you in charge of this committee?' demanded Leandra.

Alexander sighed. 'No one did,' he said. 'It just stands to reason that, as my suggestion was by far the most sensible, I should chair the meetings.'

'Why do they have to be at lunchtime?' moaned Lenny through a mouthful of tuna sandwich.

'Because,' replied Alexander, 'I wouldn't want

34

to be responsible for you missing any of your lessons.' He ignored the collective groan and pulled a small, wooden hammer out of his school bag. He tapped it on to the canteen table to get everyone's attention.

'I hereby bring the first meeting of the St Sebastian's School fête committee to order!'

James stared at the hammer. 'Where did you get that?'

'Made it in woodwork this morning,' smiled Alexander. 'Good, isn't it?'

James shook his head. 'I'm your friend, and even *I* think you're a major geek!' he said.

'Right, first order of business,' announced Alexander, carrying on despite James's comment. 'How's your punch coming along, Gordon?'

Gordon Carver grinned wickedly as he made a fist. 'Want me to show you?' he growled.

'No, it's fine!' said Alexander quickly, scanning his notes for another topic to bring up. 'I do hear, though, that you've volunteered to help Leandra with her "splat-the-rat" stall.'

'Yeah,' grunted The Gorilla. 'I've started collecting for it already!' He reached into his trouser pocket and pulled out a very dead, rather smelly rat.

Stacey Carmichael screamed and covered her face with her hands.

'What's that?' demanded Lenny.

'What does it look like?' said Gordon. 'Caught it this morning behind the bins.' He held the rat up by its tail to examine it. 'Should make a nice mess when you splat it with a hammer, this one!'

'You don't hit *real* rats!' shouted Lenny, jumping to his feet.

'It's all right!' insisted Gordon. 'They don't feel anything after I snap their necks when I catch them!' Lenny reached into his school bag and pulled out his own pet rat, Whiskers. Pulling it tight into his chest, he gently stroked the animal's patchy, grey fur.

'Oh, you've caught one, too,' said The Gorilla. 'Give it here. I'll show you how to kill it!'

Purple with rage, Lenny turned and stormed out of the canteen.

Gordon looked at the group. 'Something I said?' he asked, stuffing the dead rodent back into his pocket.

'Moving along . . .' said Alexander, tapping his hammer on the table again. 'How are the plans for the beauty pageant, Stacey?' There was no reply. Alexander sighed. 'It's all right, you can look now. The rat's gone.'

Stacey pulled her hands away from her face. 'I feel sick!' she groaned.

Turning hopefully to James, Alexander said, 'Pelt the teacher?'

'Sorted!' said James, emptying a bag of novelty bathroom sponges on to the table. One of them, in the shape of a duck, bounced into Stacey's lap. Thinking it was another rat, Stacey screamed and ran from the canteen.

'It's only a sponge!' shouted James after her, but she'd already knocked a tray of pasta into a year-nine girl's lap and pushed her way out through the double doors.

Before they stopped swinging, Lenny reappeared carrying a hastily prepared placard

that read STOP THE SLAUGHTER! 'I demand
an immediate end to the rat cull in the name of
entertainment!' he shouted.

Leandra pulled her jumper up over her head.
'He's *not* my brother!' she groaned.

Gordon roared with laughter and pulled the
rat out of his pocket again. He strode across the
canteen to dangle it in Lenny's face.

'Well,' said James, taking the small, wooden
hammer from an open-mouthed Alexander and
tapping it on the table. 'I reckon that's meeting
postponed!'

CHAPTER 5
FROM FUNFAIR TO UNFAIR

Edith held the end of a thick, white rope against one edge of the sewer tunnel. 'Get the other end!' she screeched.

Ambrose Harbottle, wary of further bullying, jumped to attention and did as he was told.

'Hang on a minute,' he said as he pressed the end of the stiff, white cord to the sewer wall. 'This isn't a rope – it's someone's spine!'

'Yes,' a cry echoed out from the other side of the amphitheatre. 'It's mine!'

'It may surprise you to know that, even as a long-standing member of the undead, I don't actually own a real tape measure!' snarled Edith, taking the end of the spine from Ambrose and making a mental note of how wide the tunnel was.

'What's all this in aid of?' asked another ghost, Bertram Ruttle, wandering over to the pair.

'Edith's found herself a new barrel,' said Ambrose flatly.

'Not just "a new barrel",' grinned Edith, her teeth crawling with maggots. 'An object of pure beauty that will transform this dump into the most desirable residence the deceased have ever seen!'

Ambrose and Bertram glanced around the underground cave. Apart from a few rats and the odd spider, the only other occupants were a pair of elderly spirits playing chess with rotting body parts. One of the old men coughed hard and launched an ectoplasmic lung on to the board. 'I'll use that for a bishop!' he announced.

'It's got to be some barrel if it can make this pit look attractive,' said Bertram.

'What is it you want?' snapped Edith.

Bertram gestured to the length of spine. 'Have you finished with that?' he asked. 'I've got a rehearsal with the Plague Pit Junior Ghost Band in a few minutes, and the neck of our double bass has snapped. That backbone would make a great replacement.'

'Take it and leave me alone!' hissed Edith, thrusting the spine into Bertram's hands. 'But if I hear one more song about me being old, ugly or "particularly warty from a certain angle", your death won't be worth living!'

'Of course not!' lied Bertram, deciding to find a better hiding place for the lyrics he wrote. 'We're working on a song called "Ode to Odour".'

'That sounds like fun,' said Ambrose, ignoring Edith's expression of annoyance. 'How does it go?'

Bertram cleared his throat. 'We've always known how much you smell, but did you know you leak as well . . .' he sang. Edith lunged out an arm and grabbed him by the throat, turning his song into a strangled gurgle.

'If that's about me . . .' she warned.

Bertram shook his head. 'We've written it for William. He's going to teach it to whoever turns out to be the jester he requested for the school fête.'

Looking back later, Ambrose decided that was the moment when he should have turned and run away. But he didn't. He stood, rooted to the spot, as Edith exploded.

'The school *what*?!' she bellowed, her fingers sinking into the ghostly goo inside Bertram as she gripped his throat.

'Did I say school fête?' he squeaked. 'I meant at the Edith-Is-Great party we're all planning!'

Edith pulled Bertram's face close to her own. 'If you don't tell me exactly what's going on, I'll tear you into enough pieces to make a dozen brand-new chess sets for those two crumblies over there!'

Despite Edith's grip on his throat, Bertram swallowed hard.

William tore another strip of green mould from the sewer-pipe wall and fed it to the Headless Horseman's horse.

'It's going to be brilliant!' the young ghost enthused. 'They're having food and drinks, and a stall where you have to throw tiny arrows into a circular board to win prizes!'

The horseman looked up from his task of replacing one of the horse's shoes, his head balanced precariously on his shoulders. 'Maybe Colin and I could go up there and offer pony rides?' he suggested.

'Who's Colin?' asked William.

The horseman gestured to his horse. 'This is Colin,' he said.

William stared at the animal. 'Why would you give one of the most terrifying creatures ever to exist in ghostly history a name like that?' he asked.

The Headless Horseman shrugged. 'He looks like a Colin.'

Before William could respond, he heard voices and the sound of feet splashing through puddles in the sewer. Ambrose and Bertram rounded the corner, out of breath.

'She's coming!' warned Ambrose.

'Who?' asked the horseman.

William took one look at the finger impressions left in Bertram's neck. 'Edith,' he said.

'I'm sorry!' said Bertram, rubbing at his throat. 'It just slipped out!'

'Don't worry,' said William. 'She was bound to find out about the school fête sooner or later.'

'But she knows you're taking part,' said Ambrose. 'She knows you asked for the jester!'

'Every fête needs a jester!' said a voice.

William squinted and could just make out the

shape of Edith standing in the shadows.

'Y-you don't mind?' he stammered.

'Of course not!' said Edith, stepping into view.
'We've been at odds with St Sebastian's for far
too long. Now is the time to make the most of
our relationship! What other ideas do we have
for this fête?'

The other ghosts glanced at each other
uncertainly. 'I, er . . . I was just saying I could
give pony rides,' said the horseman, ready to leap
on to Colin's back and gallop off at the first sign
of violence.

'Superb!' smiled Edith. 'The little darlings will
adore that!' The horseman relaxed his grip on
Colin's reins, but not much.

'I could make some leech wine,' suggested
Ambrose, not wanting to be on the wrong side if
Edith's loyalties really had changed.

'Wonderful!' grinned the hag. She gasped with
delight as another idea struck. 'And I could dress

47

up and tell the fortunes of those who come to visit the fête!'

William began to nod nervously, and was soon joined by the other ghosts in his cautious approval.

'Well, what are we waiting for?' announced Edith, clapping her hands. 'The St Sebastian's School fête deserves our undivided attention! Off you all go and make preparations!'

'Are, er . . . are you OK?' asked Ambrose.

'Never better!' replied Edith. 'Now, you get started on your leech wine, and I'll begin to put my fortune-teller's costume together!' She watched as the horseman led Colin away along the sewer pipe, followed by a stunned Ambrose, William and Bertram. As the ghosts disappeared into the darkness, Edith began to cackle.

'I don't need a costume to tell your future, you gullible ghosts!' she sneered. 'I shall use your ideas for the school fête to wreak havoc upon St Sebastian's and its pupils! I shall rain destruction upon anyone who dares set foot at this pathetic event. The sewers will run with the tears of those who have dared to disturb me! No one who buys a ticket to the fête shall be spared my fury.'

Edith Codd struck a powerful pose, the effect lessened slightly by the fact that her right foot was plunged into a mound of ghostly horse poo. 'I shall make this a fête worse than death!'

CHAPTER 6
DO NOT DISTURB

Mr Tick stared at his computer screen and sighed. How on earth was he supposed to practise for the upcoming solitaire finals in Norwich if people kept disturbing him? Despite his annoyance, the pink bunny baby monitor rigged up in place of an intercom kept buzzing.

'Yes?' he snapped, pressing a button to silence the noise. The school secretary's voice rang out of the tinny speaker.

'It's Mr Thomas again,' said Miss Keys. 'He says that, in addition to all his props for the school play, the costumes and scenery have now disappeared too.'

The headmaster sighed. 'And does he have any suspicions as to who the culprits may be?'

There was a slight pause. 'He thinks it's Graham Mucintyre, sir.'

Mr Tick stuck a finger in his ear and tried to free the lump of wax that was obviously hampering his hearing. 'I'm sorry, Miss Keys,' he said. 'For a moment I thought you said "Graham Macintyre".'

'I did, sir.'

'Graham Macintyre, the top London theatre producer?'

'Yes, sir.'

Mr Tick felt a headache coming on. 'Let me get this straight,' he said. 'Mr Thomas thinks that Graham Macintyre — the most successful producer in the history of British theatre — has nicked the costumes for a school play?'

'And the set and the props, sir,' said Miss Keys through the baby monitor. 'He's claiming that Mr Macintyre is jealous of his theatrical vision and has arranged for everything to be stolen in order to wreck the forthcoming production of *I Was a Vampire eBayer*.'

Mr Tick pinched the bridge of his nose. This wasn't just a headache; it was going to be a migraine. 'Has Graham Macintyre ever *been* to Grimesford, Miss Keys?'

'Not that I'm aware of, sir.'

The headmaster glanced at the active game of solitaire on his computer monitor and sighed as the seconds ticked away. Eventually, he leant forwards and pressed the pink bunny.

'Kindly inform Mr Thomas that, unless he stops whining, he'll cast his next play from the people he meets in the queue for unemployment benefit,' he said.

'And the props and costumes?' asked Miss Keys.

'Oh, it'll just be a prank by some of the pupils. Get Mr Wharpley to search the grounds for them!'

Suddenly, the door to the office burst open and the caretaker hurried in. 'I'll do no such thing!' he insisted. 'I've got far too much to do without wasting time hunting round for a few bits of poxy scenery!'

'Mr Wharpley,' growled the headmaster, 'whatever happened to the tradition of knocking before you enter an office?'

'Whatever happened to the tradition of hiring fairground rides that are health and safety approved?' countered Mr Wharpley.

'Very well,' said Mr Tick, scowling, 'what can I do for you?'

'It's this ghost train you've got me building on the cheap,' said Mr Wharpley loudly, making the headmaster wince. 'I want to know if –'

'Stop!' shouted a voice. 'You can't go in there!'

What now? thought Mr Tick, as he looked past the caretaker and out into Miss Keys's office. The secretary was trying to stop Lenny and a handful of other pupils from getting into his office.

'What is going on out here?' demanded Mr Tick as he appeared in the doorway, all hope of finishing his game of solitaire lost. What was the point of getting the pupils to do everything for the school fête if they insisted on involving him?

'I demand that you sign our petition to stop Gordon Carver using real rats for the splat-the-rat stall!' demanded Lenny to a chorus of cheers from his small band of supporters. 'The murdering must end!' He thrust his STOP THE SLAUGHTER! placard under Mr Tick's nose to prove his determination.

'What *is* that stench?' said Mr Tick.

'Someone's drawn pictures of rats being squished on my placard,' said Lenny, gesturing

to the brown, runny images scribbled around
his slogan, 'and I don't think they've used
felt-tip pens.'

Mr Tick began to retreat into his office. 'I will
sign no petitions,' he said. 'And I must insist that
you dispose of that placard; it's a danger to
public health!'

The pupils behind Lenny began to voice their disapproval of the headmaster's decision.

Mr Tick stepped further back as Miss Keys's telephone rang. Covering her free ear against the shouts of the children around her, she listened for a second, then called out over the din: 'It's Mr Thomas again! He thinks Steven Spielberg may have photocopied his script!'

Mr Tick started to close his office door, desperate to escape from the chaos in front of him. The door wouldn't move: Mr Wharpley was in the way.

'About this ghost train,' he insisted loudly. 'Can I chop the tombola drum in half and use it as a carriage?' He thrust a blurred photograph of the barrel into Mr Tick's hand in case he had forgotten what a work of art the drum was.

'Yes!' bellowed Mr Tick, leaning against his office door. 'Do what you want with it. Just get out of my office!'

Satisfied, Mr Wharpley stepped out of the way and the door suddenly slammed shut. Mr Tick fell flat on his face.

As he clambered to his feet and brushed down his suit, his eyes fell on the photograph of the tombola drum. 'That really is the most disgusting thing I've ever seen!' he said aloud.

On the other side of the school, someone who thought the tombola drum was the most beautiful thing she had ever seen was busy collecting ingredients for a very special recipe.

Edith was in the science-lab store cupboard gathering items that, according to the plague pit's resident witch Aggie Malkin, would create a punch drink that would have everyone running to the toilet for days.

Her plans to attack the school fête were

coming along swimmingly. She had those
ridiculous ghosts preparing for a variety of stalls
that, with a little help from her, would add to the
carnage. Ambrose's leech wine would be spiked
with thistles, she had already stitched a number
of rude words into the jester costume, and a
quick kick up the rear would ensure that Colin

the horse would end his one and only pony ride bucking like a rodeo steer.

She'd even found time to capture sewer rats and throw them into the traps set by that Carver boy. Apparently, he wanted to gather together real rodents and hit them with a hammer. Now there was a child after her own heart.

Of course, some nosy do-gooder had tried to stop Gordon, but Edith had shown what she thought of him by using filth from the sewer floor to draw crushed rats on the little angel's placard. She was slightly worried that the boy would recognise the source of the brown goo but, if he had, he hadn't said anything to his equally nosy friends.

As she plucked more and more ingredients from the store cupboard's shelves, Edith Codd began to sing new lyrics to Bertram's song, 'Ode to Odour': 'One glass of this and boy, you'll smell – one more and you'll leak as well . . .'

CHAPTER 7
TODAY'S THE DAY

Mr Wharpley squirted another dollop of hair cream into his hand and massaged it into his quiff to protect his rock 'n' roll hairstyle against the light drizzle falling outside.

Gazing at his reflection in the window of the English room, he smiled. As the fête was taking place on a Saturday, no one had to wear a uniform and, for Mr Wharpley, that meant a pink, 1950s' teddy-boy suit instead of his usual dirty brown overalls.

The caretaker swivelled his hips in a way that

he hoped would make him look like his hero, Elvis Presley but, in reality, made it appear that he badly needed the toilet. A bone cracked noisily in his leg and, swivelling abandoned, Mr Wharpley turned to head for the sports field and his home-made ghost train.

'What a wonderful day!' bellowed a voice, causing Mr Wharpley to jump backwards, cracking a bone in his other leg. Miss Keys was standing right behind him, and she appeared to be in fancy dress.

The school secretary was wearing tight, black leggings that made her lower half look as though she was trying to smuggle several kilos of mashed potatoes. Yellow trainers and a purple tie-dyed T-shirt with a picture of a silver unicorn completed the ensemble, but it was her hair that really amazed the caretaker.

Carefully back-combed, and adding at least another metre to her height, Miss Keys's hair was streaked with blue and green dye and tied with an orange bow. She looked as though she'd been given an electric shock then fallen into a pool of melted crayons.

'So, how does it work?' said Miss Keys as she and Mr Wharpley walked across the damp grass towards the ghost train. The caretaker pulled open the door to what was essentially a garden shed covered with bits of scenery from Mr Thomas's school play.

'I've rigged up the motor from an old lawnmower,' explained Mr Wharpley, as Miss Keys stepped inside and sat in one half of what had been the green tombola drum. 'That pulls on a chain which drags the carriage you're now sitting in through the assorted exhibits.' He gestured up to a variety of plastic bats and vampire capes that were nailed to the ceiling.

Miss Keys suspected that the ride would last approximately six seconds and be about as scary as a lump of cheese, but she didn't want to hurt Mr Wharpley's feelings so she pulled a face and pretended to scream. 'How terrifying!' she said.

Delighted that his invention was a hit, Mr Wharpley held out a hand to help Miss Keys out of the car and led her away from the ghost train and off to examine the remaining stalls. Had

they turned back, they might have noticed a small cloud of green gas hissing from beneath the folds of one of the black vampire capes.

Fully formed, Edith watched the oddly matched couple as they walked away. 'You don't know just how terrifying it's going to be!' she cackled.

'No way!'

'But you're the only one who fits into the costume,' said Leandra.

Alexander shook his head. 'Not in a million years!'

'What's the problem?' James asked. 'You'd make a great court jester!'

Alexander stared at his friend. 'I am a man of science,' he insisted. 'In fact, I have here in my bag my entry for the science contest – a prototype ghost-catcher! I will not have my academic image sullied by appearing as a common clown!'

'Who made this costume anyway?' asked Stacey, as she turned the rough material over in her hands. She spotted the stitching on the back. 'And what's a "crook-pated scut"?'

'It's a medieval insult meaning a thick-headed idiot,' said Alexander, 'which is another reason why I won't be wearing that ridiculous outfit.'

'It's a shame,' said James, nudging Lenny to get his attention. 'I mean, if I were somebody who'd spent the last five years compiling the world's biggest computer database of jokes, I'd jump at the chance to test them out.'

'So would I,' said Lenny, catching on. 'After all, what's the point of jokes if you don't have an audience to hear them?'

Slowly, Alexander reached out and took the jester costume from Stacey's hands. 'You know,' he said, 'we scientists aren't without our sense of humour. Einstein was noted for his practical jokes and, by all accounts, Newton was a laugh a minute!'

'That's the spirit!' said Leandra.

'We'll help you put the costume on!' suggested Stacey.

Alexander's cheeks turned deep red. 'You will not!' he said, marching off in the direction of the boys' toilets.

It was Lenny's turn to nudge James. 'Bet you wish the costume fitted you now!' he teased. James opened and closed his mouth a few times but, as Stacey smiled at Lenny's joke, he couldn't think of anything to say other than 'bluh-bluh-bluh', so he hurried off to check if his pelt-the-teacher sponges were wet enough.

'I say, I say, I say,' quipped Alexander into the mirror as he pulled the jester costume over his head, 'what does a magician keep up his sleeve?' He left a pause for his imaginary audience to reply, then answered: 'His arm!'

The boys' toilets was somewhere that Alexander would ordinarily never dream of getting changed, but this was the opportunity he'd been waiting for: the chance to unleash his latest collection of jokes upon the world.

Alexander had been collecting puns and gags for years, and spent hours each night compiling them in a comedy database. Unfortunately, his school friends had never seemed that interested in hearing any of them – until now, that is. His moment had come, and he hoped it would prove to be even more impressive than his entry for the science contest.

Costume on, Alexander posed and tried another joke on for size. 'How do goldfish access their emails? They use the fin-ternet!'

As he grinned at himself in the mirror, he

thought he saw a puff of green smoke appear over the top of one of the toilet cubicles behind him.

Tiptoeing across the room, he cautiously pushed open the door. The cubicle was empty. Leaning closer to the toilet, he peered into the bowl and saw . . . nothing. Nothing but water.

'You're letting the excitement of the moment get to you, Stick,' he scolded himself. 'Now get out there and be funny. Your audience awaits!'

CHAPTER 8
SQUEEEEEZE

'We've always known how much you smell . . .' sang the Plague Pit Junior Ghost Band as they trailed through the sewer pipe behind Bertram. 'But did you know you leak as well . . .'

William raised a hand to stop the ghosts. 'This is it,' he said.

Ambrose peered into the old iron pipe that led up from the sewer. 'You're certain this one leads to the sports field?' he asked.

William nodded. 'It comes out in the area where the teachers store their metal horses,' he replied, picturing the staff car park above them.

'It doesn't look very inviting,' moaned the Headless Horseman, swivelling his head round to turn away from the blackness of the pipe. 'Colin won't go up there.'

'Well, there's no other way,' said William. 'If we split up, we might get caught. We're better off sticking together.'

'Right,' said Ambrose, pushing his way through the group. 'I'll lead the way.'

'Oh, no,' proclaimed William, pressing a hand to Ambrose's chest to stop him. 'You've been wolfing down those high-fibre brown leeches all morning. You can go at the back where you won't do any harm!'

'What do you mean?' asked Ambrose, innocently.

William sighed. 'Let's just say that, even on a diet of sewer mould, Colin smells nicer than you.'

Ambrose gasped. 'Are you referring to . . .' He

lowered his voice to a whisper. '. . . bottom burps?'

The Plague Pit Junior Ghost Band erupted into laughter.

'Your insides are made of ectoplasm,' said William. 'I don't know much about the human body, but I've sat in on enough biology classes upstairs to know that you need a stomach to digest all the leeches you eat. Yours decomposed long ago and so, well, the combination of these two factors means you pong a bit, that's all!'

Ambrose turned away from the other ghosts and folded his arms. 'Right,' he snapped. 'If that's how you feel about me, I'm not going!'

William nudged his older friend. 'And let all that delicious leech wine go to waste?' he asked, gesturing to the bottles of potent liquid dangling from Ambrose's belt.

'I'll drink it myself!'

'Come on,' said William. 'You should be proud of yourself. None of us has mastered the art of eating since we died, let alone perfected the skill of farting!'

A ripple of laughter echoed through the Junior Ghost Band at the word.

'You mean . . . I can do things that other ghosts can't?' asked Ambrose.

'Oh, yes!' chuckled William.

Ambrose considered the news and a smile fought its way on to his lips. 'I'll go at the back.'

'OK,' said William to the entire group. 'I'll go first, followed by the horseman and Colin. Then Bertram and the band.'

'I'll be at the rear!' announced Ambrose proudly, letting out a rasp of gas that had the children giggling again.

Ten minutes later, William slipped his toes through a rusty hole in the old pipe and used it to push himself up. This was nowhere near as easy as changing shape and wriggling through the water pipes to one of the school toilets – especially when you were helping to pull a fully grown ghost horse up behind you.

Beneath Colin, the Headless Horseman and Bertram were pushing hard, forcing the creature up through the pipe. The musical spirit was sweating drops of ectoplasm as he pressed hard with his shoulder against the horse's hindquarters, desperately hoping that Ambrose was the only bottom-burper around.

The Plague Pit Junior Ghost Band followed next, instruments made from bones and decaying body parts tucked into their matching uniforms, thoroughly enjoying this unexpected adventure.

Ambrose climbed at the back of the group. He had a leech in each hand and was using them as sucker pads, splatting them in turn against the inside of the pipe and pulling himself up. When

74

one of the leeches became too gooey to stick, he popped it into his mouth and pulled a replacement from his waistcoat pocket.

Halfway up the pipe, William stopped and was rewarded with a jab from a terrified horse's nose from behind.

'What's the matter?' called Bertram around Colin. 'Why have we stopped?'

'Edith,' said William.

'She's here?' asked the horseman. He was terrified that if Edith had changed her mind about helping out at the fête and caught him on his way up to the surface without permission, Colin would be confiscated and he'd have to find something else to ride. The Headless Frogman just didn't have the same ring to it.

'No, she's not here,' William assured him. 'I've just realised that I haven't seen her today.'

'I like days like that,' echoed Ambrose's voice from further down the pipe.

'She said that she was working on her fortune-teller's costume, but I would have thought she'd have checked how everyone else was getting on.' William thought hard for a moment. 'I don't trust her.'

'I wouldn't trust her as far as I could throw her,' said Bertram.

'How far could you throw her?' asked the horseman.

'I don't know,' came the reply. 'But I bet it would be fun trying.'

'It's no use. We'll have to split up and look for her,' William decided.

'What, all of us?' questioned the horseman.

'No. You, Colin and I will continue to the surface. There's no point getting a horse this far then lowering it back down. Bertram, you take the band and search the sewers for Edith.'

Once again, Ambrose's voice bounced up the length of pipe. 'What about me?' he asked, his question followed by a loud, rasping noise.

William clamped his free hand over his mouth. 'You just stay away from any naked flames!'

CHAPTER 9
AND THEY'RE OFF!

'This is Rick Shaw, reporting for *Grimesford Today*,' smarmed the reporter, turning slightly to the left so the TV camera would get a better view of his blond highlights glinting in the weak sunshine. 'And we're at St Sebastian's School for what we're hoping will be a school fête to remember!'

'We already have a winner in the pie-eating contest,' continued Rick Shaw, gesturing to someone just out of shot to his right. 'Let's see if we can get a word with the new champion . . .' A rather green-looking Lenny stumbled into view.

'Your name, please?' said Rick Shaw, smiling broadly and revealing as many perfect white teeth as possible.

'Lenny Maxwell,' mumbled Lenny, clutching at his swollen stomach.

'And exactly how many pies did you have to eat to win the contest?'

Lenny's face turned a paler shade of green as the subject of food was mentioned. 'Twenty-seven,' he moaned.

'Wow!' enthused Rick Shaw. 'Twenty-seven pies in one sitting! That's incredible! And what flavours were they?'

Lenny swallowed hard as beads of sweat began to appear on his forehead. 'Apple, blackberry, rhubarb, ham and egg –' Suddenly he doubled over and fell out of shot.

'Cut!' yelled the cameraman. 'It's OK, Rick,' he announced to the horrified reporter with a smirk. 'We can go back and cut in just before the kid was sick on your shoes!'

'Now, remember,' said William to the Headless Horseman as he pulled the manhole cover back in place in the staff car park, 'the visitors to the fête aren't expecting ghosts today, so you'll have to appear to them as something a little more pleasant.'

The horseman glanced at the weeping sores that covered Colin's hide, then down at the tattered riding outfit he had been buried in. He nodded, closed his eyes and concentrated. 'How about this?' he asked.

William stood up and turned, wiping the leaked motor oil that coated the manhole cover from his hands. Standing beside him was a dashing hero in a highwayman's costume and a tall, proud stallion whose mane shimmered silver in the light rain.

'Incredible!' said William, concentrating to turn himself into a smart stable boy. 'You'd never know you were a ghost!'

'I thank you,' announced the horseman, taking a deep bow. He stayed bent over as his head fell off and rolled under the science teacher's hatchback car.

'You *might* want to do something about that, however,' said William.

'Ugh!' yelled Mr Tick, as yet another wet sponge hit him squarely in the face. He pulled against the rope that held him firmly in the set of stocks year ten had made in their woodwork class. 'How long must I endure this humiliation?'

'Now, now, sir,' said James as he took a pound

coin from a year-eight pupil and gestured to a bucket full of sopping sponges. 'This is all for the good of the school, and you do want to be seen to be doing your bit, don't you?'

Mr Tick disappeared briefly beneath another hail of wet sponges. 'Yes, yes!' he spluttered. 'But why does there have to be such a long queue? Mr Parker didn't attract half as many pupils.'

James shrugged and struggled to hide a smile. 'I guess you're just popular, sir!' He turned to collect money from the next in line. 'Mr Wharpley! Back again?' he said. 'Your third time, isn't it?'

'It is,' grinned the caretaker wickedly, as he pulled a number of heavy, industrial cleaning pads from the pocket of his teddy-boy jacket. 'And this time, I've brought my own sponges!'

Unable to bear Mr Tick's panicked cries of protest, Miss Keys hurried away from the pelt-the-teacher stall and over to the refreshments table. She dipped a plastic cup into the jug of punch. Raising it to her lips, she stopped.

The punch smelt, well . . . different. Certainly not like the cranberry surprise the headmaster had been hoping for. More like . . . what *was* that smell? That was it! More like the old lab coats she had been stitching in her office. The punch smelt like science-lab chemicals.

As she stared into the deep red liquid, wondering whether to take a sip, Stacey Carmichael paraded past wearing a tiara and a sash that proclaimed her to be Fête Beauty Queen. The fact that no one else had bothered to enter the contest didn't seem to worry her.

'Oh, Miss Keys!' she said, spotting the secretary and dashing over. 'They think I'm beautiful!'

Miss Keys opened her mouth to reply, but her words were drowned out by a terrible scream from the home-made ghost train. Stacey jumped at the sound, sending both her and the school secretary crashing into the refreshment table and spilling the bowl of punch all over the pair.

'My hair!' yelled Stacey as the chemicals mixed into the drink began to react with the extra-shine hairspray she had smothered herself with before the beauty contest.

Miss Keys watched in horror as Stacey's hair began to fizzle and melt. Grabbing a bottle of

ketchup from the hot-dog trolley next to the ruined table, she aimed squirt after squirt of the sticky sauce all over Stacey's head.

'What are you doing?' screamed Stacey, as the ketchup began to dribble down her face.

'Saving your beauty title!' snapped Miss Keys, grabbing a bottle of mustard and adding it to the rescue effort.

As she and Stacey struggled in the remains of the food table, the door to the ghost train finally burst open and a young mother raced out, still screaming and dragging her six-year-old boy across the grass. The lad was grinning madly. 'That was cool!' he shouted. 'Again! Again!'

On the far side of the sports field, the screaming mother attracted William's attention. 'Get me over there!' he said to the Headless Horseman.

The horseman, head now firmly in place thanks to an entire roll of sticky tape, reached

down and scooped William up into the saddle of the powerful stallion that was Colin. They galloped across the field, leaping gracefully over Miss Keys and Stacey to land next to the ghost train.

William glanced back at the terrified mother, now being comforted by Ms Legg, the PE teacher. 'This is Edith's work,' he growled.

'E-Edith?' stammered the horseman, forgetting to concentrate on being a dashing highwayman. Within seconds, he'd turned back into a rotting corpse beside an old, decaying horse. The surprise caused William to change back from a stable boy to a scrawny plague victim.

Silence filled the school fête. A girl gasped and the horseman spun round to look at her. The sticky tape that was holding the two halves of his neck together gave way, and his head bounced to the ground.

Then the chaos began.

CHAPTER 10
DON'T PANIC!

Screams echoed out across the sports field, attracting the attention of Rick Shaw and his cameraman. 'Something's happening,' barked the reporter, 'follow me!' The pair abandoned the bemused winner of the knobbly knees contest and ran towards the source of the chaos. Everything seemed to be centred around the ghost train.

William glanced over at the horseman's body as it stumbled around, searching for its skull. He knew what he had to do.

'Sorry!' he said, then he kicked the horseman's head as hard as he could.

Rick Shaw could see figures outside the ghost train now. There was a boy dressed in rags, a rather scrawny horse, and there was a man with them who seemed to be missing a –

Hearing the scream, Rick Shaw looked up just in time to see the horseman's wide-eyed face before it cracked against his own, head-butting the reporter and knocking him out cold. The cameraman, trying to run and film at the same time, tripped over his colleague and crashed to the ground, smashing several thousand pounds' worth of TV camera in the process.

William allowed himself a brief smile, but soon realised his actions had made things worse. The visitors to the fête who, until now had merely been scared by the sight of some spooky-looking characters, had now witnessed the ghosts attack a local celebrity. They started to fight back.

'Colin, focus!' shouted the horseman, but it was too late. Spotting the remains of the refreshment stand in the distance and, in particular, the tasty-looking meal that was Stacey's ketchup-and-mustard-covered hair, he blew through his nostrils and galloped away.

Feeling vulnerable, William looked around quickly for another hiding place. He spotted the open door to the ghost train and shouted: 'In there!'

'Where?' yelled the horseman.

William pulled his head from his shoulders and aimed its eyes towards the decorated shed. 'There!'

It was dark inside the ghost train.

'It's dark inside this ghost train,' said the Headless Horseman.

'Shhh!' warned William. 'I'm pretty sure Edith's in here somewhere!'

The horseman swallowed hard, which wasn't easy to do as his head was tucked under his arm and he ended up dribbling down his trousers.

'I can seeeeee youuuuuu!' sang a reedy voice in the blackness.

William would have known that voice anywhere. 'Edith, you have to stop this!' he shouted over the muffled sounds of pandemonium from outside. 'People are going to get hurt!'

'And why should I be worried about that?' sneered the darkness.

'Because you care about people,' replied William. 'You care about us – the plague-pit ghosts! You've been battling for years to close the school so that we can finally rest in peace!'

William stumbled blindly through the blackness of the ghost train, arms outstretched in case he tripped or found a wall. 'Those people out there are just like us,' he said.

'They're NOT like us!' screamed Edith from her hiding place. 'They're alive! They have a future! And what do I have to look forward to? Eternity with a bunch of ungrateful spirits!' There was a sudden rumble and William felt the air move as the ghost-train car containing Edith shot past him in the darkness.

'We are grateful, Edith,' he shouted. 'We just don't think you should be attacking the pupils and staff. Isn't that right, horseman?'

'Don't bring me into this!' the horseman pleaded.

William sighed. 'Come out, Edith, or at least turn the lights on so we can talk.'

'There's nothing to talk about!' screeched Edith. 'By tomorrow morning, St Sebastian's will be in ruins!' The tombola-carriage sped past again and a replica battleaxe swung out of the shadows and whizzed over William's head. Had the Headless Horseman been wearing his, it would have been sliced off again. A whimper came from beneath his arm.

'Edith!' bellowed William. 'Give up now! Don't force me to stop you!'

'You?' cackled Edith. 'What can you do? You're nothing but a farm boy; a peasant who amounted to nothing in life, and has done precious little with his death!'

William took a deep breath. 'I might surprise you, Edith!' he said.

The ghost-train car shot past again and Edith slapped the young ghost across the back of the head. 'Go on, then, peasant boy!' she teased. 'Surprise me!'

William had been listening to the sound of the carriage as it rumbled round the track in the blackness, timing it as it made each circuit of the small shed. He concentrated as the sound of the

metal wheels grew louder then, at the right
moment, leapt forwards and pushed the car off
its track.

Edith crashed to the floor, screaming. She
pulled herself out of the carriage and ran her
hands across it, lovingly. 'My barrel!' she
screeched. 'My beautiful barrel!'

Her head snapped up and her eyes began to glow red. William and the horseman were lit by two scarlet laser beams.

'That's it!' squeaked the horseman. 'I'm off!' Grabbing his head, he shoved it down the back of his trousers so that he couldn't see Edith any longer.

That just left William. As the red-eyed, furious ghost crept over the derailed barrel towards him, the young ghost held his breath. This wasn't going to be pleasant.

CHAPTER 11
JESTER MINUTE

'Get me out of here!' yelled Mr Tick as James struggled with the stocks that were holding the headmaster secured to the pelt-the-teacher stall.

'I'm trying!' said James. 'The key's wet and my hands are slipping!'

'You'll have plenty of time to practise opening padlocks during a whole year of detentions if you don't release me immediately!' bellowed Mr Tick.

James sighed and wiped his hands on his trousers before trying again. This time, the lock opened with a click. Glaring at his former captor, Mr Tick turned and ran off through the chaos of the fête.

James scanned the panicky crowd for a friendly face. Spotting Lenny emerging from the main building, he dropped the key back into his bag and raced over.

'We've got to do something!' he shouted as he reached his friend. 'The ghosts are behind this!'

'Muh!' groaned Lenny, easing himself to the ground and leaning back against the wall of the school.

'Muh?' repeated James. 'What's "Muh"?'

'Don't feel well,' said Lenny, weakly. 'Too many pies.'

'Never mind that!' snapped James. 'We've got to do something!' He grabbed Lenny's wrist and tried to pull him to his feet but his friend just slid down and pressed his face against the cold, wet concrete of the playground.

'Lenny! I saw some ghosts go into the ghost train. We have to keep them trapped in there!' James's eyes widened as an idea hit him. 'Trap the ghosts ... That's it!' Turning, he sprinted back towards the sports field and the science invention contest.

Face down on the playground, Lenny wished his friend luck: 'Muh!'

James reached the table that displayed the submissions for the scientific invention contest. Much to his dismay, Alexander's prototype ghost-catcher hadn't been the only entry.

He was surprised to find the school science teacher, Mr Watts, calmly judging the entries with another woman. 'Ah, James,' he said. 'I'd like you to meet Miss Tube, head of science at St Mary's School. She's our independent judge for the contest.'

'But, sir . . .' began James, gesturing to the chaos behind him. Terrified parents were searching for screaming children while dozens of pupils tried to outrun the rampaging ghostly horse.

'Oh, that,' said Mr Watts dismissively with a wave of his hand. 'There's no such thing as ghosts. Scientific minds such as our own know there must be a rational explanation for whatever's causing the mass hysteria.' He turned to his fellow boffin. 'Now, Tess, what do you think of this automatic leg-slicer invented by Wayne Middlemiss of year eight?'

James's patience was wearing thin. The plague-pit ghosts were attacking the school again and here he was talking to quite possibly the two most insane people at the fête; they didn't even have the sense to run away!

His eyes scanned the range of odd-looking machines that filled the table. The devices had wires, aerials and even spoons sticking out of them – but there was nothing to say which one was the prototype ghost-catcher.

'Which invention,' he demanded as politely as he could, 'is Alexander Tick's?'

'Now, now,' said Mr Watts, wagging a finger, 'I know Alexander is a friend of yours, but a "ghost-catcher" is simply not a scientific invention, seeing as spirits and ghouls do not actually exist.'

'Indeed not,' added Miss Tube. 'Inventions must prove their scientific worth. Even the automatic leg-slicer must stand on its own two feet!' She chortled at the weak joke and, before long, Mr Watts was laughing too. James stared at the pair, giggling away while pandemonium reigned around them.

There's only one person who can help me now, he thought. *And he's dressed as a jester!*

'Well, the reason children should be taught in an aeroplane is so that they get a higher education!' grinned Alexander. On the other side of the classroom, Mr Thomas, the drama teacher, scribbled the joke down into his notepad.

103

'This is great stuff!' he said. 'Your jokes will be perfect for next year's play – it's all about a school that is somehow magically transported to the middle of a jungle.'

'Really?' said Alexander. 'What's it called?'

Mr Thomas raised his hands in the air theatrically and announced, '*The School That Is Somehow Magically Transported to the Middle of a Jungle!*' The drama teacher's expression darkened. 'You won't tell anyone, will you?' he demanded. 'I've had enough of major film and theatre companies abusing my talents for free!'

Alexander was shaking his head when James burst into the room. 'You're a hard man to find!' he announced.

'I was just helping Mr Thomas with a few script ideas,' explained Alexander, secretly glad of the disruption.

'Well, while you two have been brainstorming,' said James, walking to the classroom window, 'look at what's been happening to the school fête!'

Alexander and Mr Thomas joined James and peered out at the wrecked stalls, runaway horse and fleeing children. 'The ghosts!' breathed Alexander. James nodded.

As the two boys sprinted out of the classroom, Mr Thomas stared sadly at the home-made ghost train. 'They wouldn't have done that to one of Graham Macintyre's sets!' he exclaimed to the empty room.

Alexander reached across the scientific invention stall and grabbed his prototype ghost-catcher. It resembled a vacuum cleaner with a clear, plastic bulb on the back.

'That's it?' asked James. 'I thought that was the automatic leg-slicer.'

'Leg-slicer?' said Alexander. 'Why would anyone invent something that sliced legs?'

'It's not always the initial use that proves the most valuable,' said Mr Watts as he checked the notes on his clipboard. 'This thing slices more than just legs.'

'Yes,' said James, as he dragged Alexander away from the stall. 'It's pretty good at cutting off a science teacher's grip on reality, too!'

Reaching the ghost train, James and Alexander paused.

'Does this ghost-catcher really work?' asked James.

Alexander shrugged. 'The theory's sound, but I've never had the opportunity to try it out for real.'

'Now's your chance,' grinned James. 'On three?'

Alexander nodded and counted with his friend: 'One, two, three!'

Both boys raised their legs in the air and kicked open the door to the ghost train. As daylight flooded the inside of the shed, the boys saw William and the horseman cowering on the floor.

Alexander studied the lump in the back of the horseman's trousers. 'Either that's where he keeps his head, or he's really scared!' he said.

Suddenly, Edith leapt into view, eyes burning red and rotten teeth bared.

'Come to be destroyed have you along with these fools, my pretties?' she screeched.

Alexander raised the nozzle of the ghost-catcher and aimed it at the disgusting hag. 'No!' he shouted. 'We've come to further the cause of scientific achievement!'

James flicked the switch.

CHAPTER 12
WE'RE CAUGHT IN A TRAP

'This is Rick Shaw, reporting for *Grimesford Today*.' The reporter, bruises on his face covered with make-up borrowed from Miss Keys, spoke into the spare camcorder his cameraman kept in the van.

'We've witnessed some incredible events here at the St Sebastian's School fête, but none quite so amazing as the story of Alexander Tick who claims to have captured a real, live – or should that be real, dead – ghost!'

Alexander stepped into view, holding up his prototype ghost-catcher, the glass dome at the end now swirling with green mist. Faint screams could be heard echoing from inside the machine and, occasionally, a burst of red sparks caused the assembled crowd to say 'Ooh!' and Rick Shaw to flinch backward for fear of further injury.

'So, young man, can you tell us exactly how this contraption works?' asked Rick Shaw, one eye on the ghost-catcher and the other on the camera.

'Well, Rick,' began Alexander, clearly enjoying his moment in the limelight, 'the reality of apparition containment has long posed problems for the scientific community. I simply converted a standard vacuum cleaner to cope with non-transparent ethereal ectoplasmic activity and, as I think we can all see, the result is one annoyed ghost!'

Rick Shaw smiled nervously into the camera. 'I'm sorry to say I didn't understand a word of that!'

Watching the interview from just out of shot, James was treated to a nudge in the ribs. A much-recovered Lenny was standing beside him. 'Now he knows how I feel,' he grinned.

'I, however, did understand what Alexander said,' announced Mr Watts as he joined the group in front of the lens. 'And, having been proven wrong about the existence of ghosts, it is my pleasure to award this brilliant young man with the St Sebastian's School science prize!'

Miss Tube produced the trophy – an oversized test tube mounted on a fake marble plinth – much to Alexander's delight. The crowd erupted into applause and Alexander was delighted to see his father clapping with them. Fighting back tears, he handed the ghost-catcher to a trembling Rick Shaw and accepted his prize.

'There are those who have mocked my interest in science,' said Alexander to the assembled crowd, 'and those who have teased my delight in jokes. Now, as I stand before you today, I can finally combine the two by revealing what we scientists like for lunch . . . Fission chips!'

'Fission chips!' roared Alexander again with delight, as Mr Tick reached into shot and pulled

his son away from the camera to a hail of
groans and hisses from the crowd. James took the
ghost-catcher from the stunned Rick Shaw.

'He doesn't get out much,' he explained.

'Fish and chips?' whispered the Headless
Horseman to William in the darkest corner of
the now-deserted ghost train. 'I don't get it.'

'I think,' said William, crouched behind the
ghost-train carriage, 'that it was meant to be
funny.' Even though he hadn't got the joke, he'd
got the jester he'd wanted. That was enough for
him.

'Right,' he said, standing. 'Time to get out of
here.'

'B-but what if they suck us up like they did
with Edith?' stammered the horseman.

William considered the problem. Edith had

screamed in agony as Alexander's machine had pulled her inside, tearing at her ectoplasm and ripping her physical shape into pieces. It certainly wasn't something he wanted to go through.

'We'll make ourselves invisible,' he said. Minutes later, unseen by anyone, William and the horseman stepped out into the fading daylight.

Staff and pupils were in the process of clearing up the fête: collecting broken exhibits and prizes and trying to piece smashed stalls back together. In the far corner of the field, Colin the horse was happily munching on the grass, clearly enjoying the change from sewer mould.

'You go and get Colin,' said William as something more interesting caught his eye. It was a jug, floating just off the ground.

'I know that's you, Ambrose,' said William as he arrived at the shattered refreshment stand.

'Blast!' moaned the leech merchant. 'I was trying to get rid of this punch before anyone noticed.'

'I told you to wait until dark!' complained another voice from the air.

'Bertram?' asked William.

The musical ghost rested an invisible hand on his shoulder. 'That's me, lad.'

'Did the Junior Ghost Band make it to the surface?'

'Not this time,' replied Bertram. 'But I've promised to write them a musical all about what happened here today. They'll be able to perform it in the amphitheatre for everyone.'

William looked back at the ghost train. Mr Thomas was rubbing his hands despairingly over the pieces of stage set nailed crudely to the outside of the shed, sobbing, 'My set! My show! My career!'

'Do me a favour?' said William. 'Make an

extra copy. I know someone who'd like that
a lot.'

Three figures stole across the playground in the
dead of night, heading for the staff car park.

'Are you sure we're doing the right thing?'
hissed Lenny.

'I'm certain,' said James. 'She might be a nasty
old hag, but we've got no right to keep her
imprisoned like this.'

'But the scientific research . . .' moaned
Alexander, his ghost-catcher clutched lovingly in
his hands. 'I could study her, experiment on her,
learn from her . . .'

Another shower of red sparks lit the boys' faces
as a tinny scream rang out from inside the
machine.

'And you could be torn limb from limb when

116

she finally escapes,' added James with a scowl. 'You said it yourself – this is a prototype. You have no idea how long you can keep a ghost stored this way and the longer she's in there, the more angry she'll get!'

'OK,' sighed Alexander. 'Let's do it.'

The trio reached the manhole in the teachers' car park and, using a crowbar borrowed from his dad's toolbox, Lenny prised up the cover and pulled it to one side. Alexander lowered the nozzle of the ghost-catcher into the black hole before them.

'Ready?' he asked, his finger hovering over the buttons on the side of the adapted vacuum cleaner.

'Ready,' confirmed James. 'Just make sure you've got it set to blow and, Lenny, as soon as she's out, get the manhole cover back on quick!'

'OK,' said Alexander. 'One, two, three!'

He pressed down hard on the 'blow' button

and, with an agonised scream that threatened to pierce the boys' eardrums, Edith was fired out of the ghost-catcher and down the pipe to the sewers.

Lenny pushed the heavy, metal cover with his feet until it clanked back into place over the manhole, cutting off the sound. The three boys sat back, staring at the now dark and silent ghost-catcher.

'I nearly had a ghost of my own to study,' said Alexander, 'but I know we did the right thing.'

James nudged him and winked. 'That's the spirit!' he quipped.

CHAPTER 13
MONEY, MONEY, MONEY

Miss Keys furiously combed her hair. It was 9.30 on Monday morning and, despite washing it repeatedly the previous day, she still couldn't get it to lie properly. What was worse, the coloured hair dyes she had thought were temporary had mixed together to turn her unruly style a bright purple. She looked like a furry plum.

'For the last time, will you leave your hair alone and finish adding up the money raised by the school fête!' yelled Mr Tick from his own office.

Miss Keys dropped her comb and tapped the final few figures into her calculator.

'There!' she said, scurrying up to the headmaster's desk and pushing it under his nose. 'More than enough for the sports and science equipment we need, *and* we can afford to fix the school roof. No more drips of rain to water down the school dinners any further than they need to be.'

'Or . . .' said Mr Tick, 'I could get this!' He whipped a computer catalogue out of his briefcase and pointed to an ad circled in red ink: 'The Solitaire six thousand: faster processor, more memory and pre-loaded with digitised solitaire cards that feature everything from the seven wonders of the world to great headmasters of our times.'

Mr Tick's eyes twinkled as he produced a second catalogue from inside the first. 'And, how do you think I would look at the Norwich solitaire finals dressed in this?' He opened the catalogue to a picture of a bright-yellow suit emblazoned with a blue ace-of-spades pattern and a red nine-of-hearts tie.

'Oh, Mr Tick!' breathed Miss Keys. 'You'd look so handsome!'

The secretary ran a finger coyly over the edge of the headmaster's desk. 'Mr Tick . . .' she began, barely drawing his attention away from the picture. 'I know that Mrs Tick doesn't accompany you to the solitaire finals . . .' She began to blush. 'Do you think . . . if it wouldn't be too much trouble, that is . . . that I might come with you this year?'

Mr Tick looked up from his catalogue at the purple-haired secretary standing on the other side of his desk.

'No, Miss Keys,' he said, flatly. 'You'd clash with my suit.'

'Who drew that?' demanded Alexander as he stared at the cartoon of himself dressed as a jester while accepting his science prize.

'If I were you,' said James, 'I'd be more worried about where The Gorilla's just stuck that drawing pin!'

'It's not fair,' moaned the headmaster's son as he, James and Lenny walked away from the noticeboard in the direction of their next lesson.

'On Saturday, I was a hero. Now, a mere two days later, no one wants to talk about the genius of my winning invention.'

'Celebrity status is a fragile thing,' said James.

A flash of silver caught the boys' attention as Stacey appeared out of a classroom further down the corridor. 'But I'm ridiculed in a drawing while Stacey's still wearing the tiara she won in the beauty contest!' moaned Alexander.

Lenny shook his head. 'She can't take it off,' he explained. 'Whatever was in that punch melted her hair into the metal. She was round at our house with Leandra yesterday, trying to find a way to remove it without shaving her head.'

'Still,' sighed Alexander, 'I at least hoped my fellow pupils would begin to respect me a little.'

James stopped. 'Answer me a question,' he said.

'OK.'

'What were you talking about with Mr Parker at the end of double maths just then?' asked James.

Alexander grinned and pulled a handful of papers out of his school bag. 'I was convincing him to give me extra homework,' he said.

James wrapped an arm around his friend's shoulder and they started walking again. 'We need to talk about this "respect from your fellow pupils" thing,' he grinned.

Mr Wharpley pulled a dirty rag out the pocket of his even dirtier caretaker's overalls and slipped an Elvis Presley disc into his aged CD player.

Mr Wharpley wiggled his hips in time with the music and threw the final item on top of the pile of broken stalls and his recently dismantled ghost train. It was the half of the lime-green tombola drum he had used for the ride's carriage.

Watching from the other side of the sports field, Edith Codd pulled her left arm back into place for the fifth time that morning and crossed her fingers. Ever since she had been sucked inside Alexander's ghost-catcher, her ectoplasm hadn't been the same. Once thick and able to hold its shape, it was now thin and runny. Edith was oozing everywhere.

'No, please don't,' she begged out loud as she

watched the caretaker approach the bonfire.
'I loved that barrel!'

But it was too late. Mr Wharpley struck a
match and set the bonfire alight, burning the old
shed and broken tables, and melting Edith's last
chance to give the amphitheatre a makeover.

A voice from behind startled her. 'One, two,
three, four . . .' It was Bertram Ruttle, counting in
the Plague Pit Junior Ghost Band, all completely
invisible. Trumpets made from hollowed-out arm
bones, ribcage xylophones and a brand-new
double bass with a spine for a neck all joined in
with the Elvis song. Edith covered her ears and
screamed.

'You know,' said Ambrose Harbottle, sitting
behind the band and choosing a leech from the
wooden case in his waistcoat pocket, 'there's
nothing like a school fête to cheer everyone up.'

The Headless Horseman, happy that Edith's
attention was firmly on the melting barrel, lifted

his head off the grass to nod in agreement as Ambrose popped the wriggling leech into his mouth and began to chew.

William appeared beside the pair. 'All done?' asked Ambrose.

'Yep,' said William. 'It wasn't easy, but we did it.'

'Do you think she'll like it?' said Ambrose as he watched Edith trying to reshape her legs from the pool of runny goo they had become.

William pictured the other half of the lime-green tombola drum he had just set up as the brand-new amphitheatre ranting post, and smiled.

'Yes,' he said. 'I think she'll love it.'

SURNAME: Keys

FIRST NAME: Pat

AGE: 46

HEIGHT: 1.4 metres

EYES: Blue

HAIR: Mousy-brown colour

LIKES: Keeping things organised; Mr Tick's dashing appearance; Mr Tick's smile; in fact, quite a few things about Mr Tick . . .

DISLIKES: Being shouted at by Mr Tick when he's angry, especially when it's not her fault

SPECIAL SKILL: Getting her own way with the headmaster - without him realising it, of course!

INTERESTING FACT: Though she would never admit it, Miss Keys rather fancies Mr Tick - it's the shiny shoes and serious frown that do it. She spends quite a lot of her time daydreaming about him behind her desk, so it upsets her when he breezes through and slams his door without saying a word!

For more facts on Pat Keys, go to **www.too-ghoul.com**

Alexander Tick's
Joke File

(page 4,207)

Q Which side of a duck has the most features on it?

A The outside!

Q What's the difference between a fireman and a soldier?

A You can't dip a fireman

Q What's black, white and hard?

A A penguin with a machine gun!

Q What do you call a man with a seagull on his head?

A Cliff!

NOTE TO SELF: input these into jokes database at earliest convenience

(Q) Why do snails have shiny shells?
(A) Cos they use snail varnish!

(Q) What has two legs and flies?
(A) Your trousers!

(Q) What colour is the wind?
(A) Blew!

(Q) Why don't lobsters share?
(A) Cos they're shellfish!

(Q) What do you get if you shut a mouse in the fridge?
(A) Mice cubes!

(Q) Why do mice need oiling?
(A) Cos they squeak!

How to Construct Your
in Six Easy* Stages

By Alexander Tick (inventor)

Congratulations! You're the proud owner of a Patent Tick Ghost-O-Suck™. Just follow these easy steps to get your Ghost-O-Suck™ up and running in no time!

STEP 1 Remove all packaging and lay out the 317 different Ghost-O-Suck™ parts. Make sure the ectoplasmic activity components (parts 219–298) are the right way up.

STEP 2 Use a soldering iron, some rubber bands, a blunt spoon and four tablespoons of flour to stick the first 164 components together. Test the apparition containment circuits by firing them simultaneously.

STEP 3 Add part 165, making sure it is screwed tightly on to the ectoplasm rebound circuit (see fig.3). Failure to get this right could lead to certain, instant, unpleasant death when you switch the Ghost-O-Suck™ on.

fig.3

Ghost-O-Suck™

*Actual stages may not be easy

Test these instructions on Lenny and James to see if the intellectually challenged can understand them.

STEP 4 Construct and affix the ectoplasmic activity circuit. If you only have an advanced degree in astrophysics you may need to get an adult to help with this part. Though really, it's very simple.

STEP 5 Add the Ghost-O-Suck™ Ghost Bag™ on to the back of part 304(b), using the apparition bonding glue provided (see fig.4). Remember to empty your Ghost Bag™ every 12 ghosts caught, to avoid a supernatural ghoulish explosion that could cause a tear in time and space, destroying the earth.

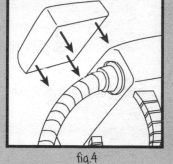

fig.4

STEP 6 Plug the Ghost-O-Suck™ into a standard power outlet and press 'go'.

Step 6 is a little unclear: maybe add illustration?

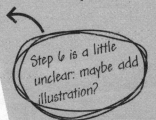

REMEMBER:

Include spectral-activity back-up circuits in final prototype

SAVE OUR RATS

Fellow pupils – our RATS are in DANGER!

YES, that's right – those lovable furry creatures that run around the canteen are being ATTACKED by ~~Gordon Carver~~ certain UNAMED BULLIES in this school, all for the benefit of the SCHOOL FÊTE.

WHAT CAN YOU DO?

See Lenny Maxwell, year seven, for details and placards. Remember – if we don't act now, we could end up with NO RATS in the canteen! NO RATS in the PE cupboard! NO RATS nibbling our toes during assembly!

JOIN THE PROTEST TO SAVE OUR RATS!

DEMONSTRATION TODAY OUTSIDE MR TICK'S OFFICE

If you can't bear to see such BEAUTIFUL creatures MURDERED under your very noses, then PROTEST! SIGN THE PETITION! WRITE TO YOUR MP!

Can't wait for the next book in the series?
Here's a sneak preview of

WHICH WITCH?

available now from all good bookshops,
or **www.too-ghoul.com**

CHAPTER 1
A BOX OF BATS

Mr Wharpley dropped his noodle snack (pickled onion and boiled egg flavour) half-eaten on to the workbench and grumbled across the cellar.

'Blimmin' kids,' he muttered. A stray piece of slimy noodle flew from between his front teeth and landed in his moustache. 'Blimmin' Halloween. Ghouls and phantoms: they'll be telling me the magic pixies really exist next.'

Hands on hips, he surveyed the pile of boxes in front of the corner cupboard. The Halloween decorations were in there somewhere. He'd thrown them there himself just under a year ago.

'That pesky Miss Keys,' he grunted. 'I bet Mr Tick would never have remembered if she hadn't reminded him. Sticking her nose in where it's not wanted.'

He scratched the back of his head, behind his ear. A fine shower of dandruff sprinkled on to the shoulders of his brown caretaker's overall. 'I'm getting too old for this. Up and down ladders like a monkey, and what thanks do I get? Don't even get to finish my dinner in peace, that's what.'

Of all the events of the year, Mr Wharpley hated Halloween especially. Even more than Christmas. Even more than – he only just stopped himself spitting at the thought of all those pink tissue-paper hearts – Valentine's Day. Because the decorations for Halloween, more than any other day, need to be hung from ceilings. Plastic bats and cobwebs and witches'

brooms and spiders: they just don't dangle the
same way from a wall.

And ceilings meant ladders. And ladders meant
only one thing to Mr Wharpley: danger. Because
the only way to not get dizzy on a ladder is to
not look down. And if you don't look down, you
don't know what's beneath you. Which is asking
for trouble.

The last time he'd been up a ladder had nearly
been the end of him. His ears turned a strange
shade of purple as he remembered: getting all the
way to the second-from-top rung before he
glanced down to see Gordon – a nasty piece of
work, that Gordon, no wonder the kids called
him 'The Gorilla' – running off with a pot of
glue dangling from his meaty paws. It had taken
half an hour of wobbly teetering to get his shoes
untied and get free.

'I'm too old for this,' he repeated. He took one
huge step over a nativity scene and one giant

leap over a pile of Diwali lanterns. 'They should pay me danger money,' he groaned.

Mr Wharpley reached the cupboard, braced himself and pulled the door open. Twenty seconds later, when the shower of paper chains, fairy lights and rolled-up banners had slowed to the occasional bounce off the top of his head, he clapped eyes on the box he'd been looking for. It was easy to spot: there was a skeleton sticking out of the top.

Stacey and Leandra had their backs to the stairs, so they didn't see him approach. And James, Alexander and Lenny were too busy looking at Stacey to notice anything much. In fact, it was only when Mr Wharpley, his vision blocked by the box and its contents, bumped into Stacey that anyone noticed he was there at all.

Glow-in-the-dark skeletons, snaggle-toothed
pumpkins, vampire bats and big hairy spiders
cascaded from the open top. A bat landed in
Stacey's hair. For a moment, everyone was
transfixed. Then Stacey reached up and touched
the bat's rubbery wings and let out a shriek that
shocked them all into action.

140

'Get it off, get it off, getitooooofffff! Eeeeee!' howled Stacey.

'Stay still!' shrieked Leandra. 'Don't move!'

James jumped forwards and started helping her untangle the bat's claws from her shiny blonde tresses.

'Aaaah, for the love of Elvis!' cursed Mr Wharpley, as a tin of spray-on cobweb fell from the box and rolled across the floor to come to a halt by Lenny's foot. 'What are you lot doing here?'

Lenny picked up the tin. 'It's lunch break, Mr Wharpley,' he said helpfully. 'Can I give you a hand?'

The back pocket of Mr Wharpley's overalls started to hiss and crackle. 'Reg? Reg? Are you there? Over.'

Glaring at Lenny, he dropped the box on the floor and felt around his backside for the walkie-talkie. 'Mr Wharpley here, over,' he said, pointedly.

'Ah, Reg,' said Miss Keys, not noticing. 'How are you getting on with those decorations?'

Mr Wharpley snorted, making the piece of noodle wobble in his moustache like a wriggly worm. Stacey stopped shrieking to watch, fascinated.

'Yeah,' he said to Lenny, ignoring Miss Keys's plaintive tones, 'you can go and get the ladder and bring it to the hall for me, if you want to be helpful.'

Lenny lolloped off down the stairs on his size tens. The caretaker thumped his thumb down on the walkie-talkie button. 'Mr Wharpley here,' he barked. 'I'm on my way.'

'So,' said Leandra to the others as her brother shambled off, 'guess what?'

'What?' asked James.

'You know the Halloween disco?'

'You could hardly miss it,' replied James, 'it's all the year-seven girls have talked about for the last week. What about it?'

'Well, guess who's in charge?'

'Albert Einstein,' said Alexander.

They all looked at him. 'Who's Albert Einstein?' asked Stacey. 'Is he in your year?'

'No,' began Alexander, 'he's a famous physicist. He coined the Theory of Relativity, "e" equals "mc" squared, which is based around the concept that energy –'

'Naah!' gurned Leandra, ignoring him. 'Me and Stacey!'

'Stacey and I,' corrected Alexander.

'No, not you and Stacey – me and Stacey,' replied Leandra.

'No, no. I mean "Stacey and I" is right,' explained Alexander.

'Look, this is a disco, not Chess Club, Stick,'

said Stacey. 'Why don't you leave it to us girls? We know what we're doing.'

Alexander sighed heavily.

'Thing is . . .' began Leandra.

'Go on,' said Alexander.

'We've got to find some volunteers. Do you know anyone who can DJ? We don't know anyone.'

The words had left James's mouth before he could stop them. 'Sure,' he replied. 'That's no problem.'

He was rewarded with a dazzling smile. From Stacey – Leandra merely rolled her eyes.

'Can you really?' asked Stacey.

'Course I can,' he heard himself saying. 'Piece of cake.'

'Did someone say cake?' said Lenny, reappearing just in time to hear the offer.

Alexander caught his friend's eye behind the girls' backs and gestured from James to Stacey.

The penny dropped, and Lenny shared a secret smirk with Alexander. James had never been near a turntable in his life. His urge to impress Stacey had got the better of him again.

'Great!' said Stacey. 'Cool! Thanks, James!'

'Any time,' he replied, confidently.

The three boys put their hands in their pockets and watched the girls walk off towards the playground, convinced they'd ticked off an item on their list.

'What on earth made you say that, James?' asked Lenny.

'He's always in a *spin* when Stacey's around,' said Alexander.

James glared. Lenny sniggered. 'Yeah,' he said. 'He gets all *mixed* up.'

Alexander sniggered back. 'Sorry, James. Just *tune* us out.'

'But seriously,' said Lenny, pulling himself together, 'how are you planning to get out of this one, James?'

James shrugged as Stacey and Leandra disappeared round the corner. 'I have absolutely no idea,' he said.